ADOPT A C

iAmMoshow's Lyrical Cat Tales

By iAmMoshow The Cat Rapper

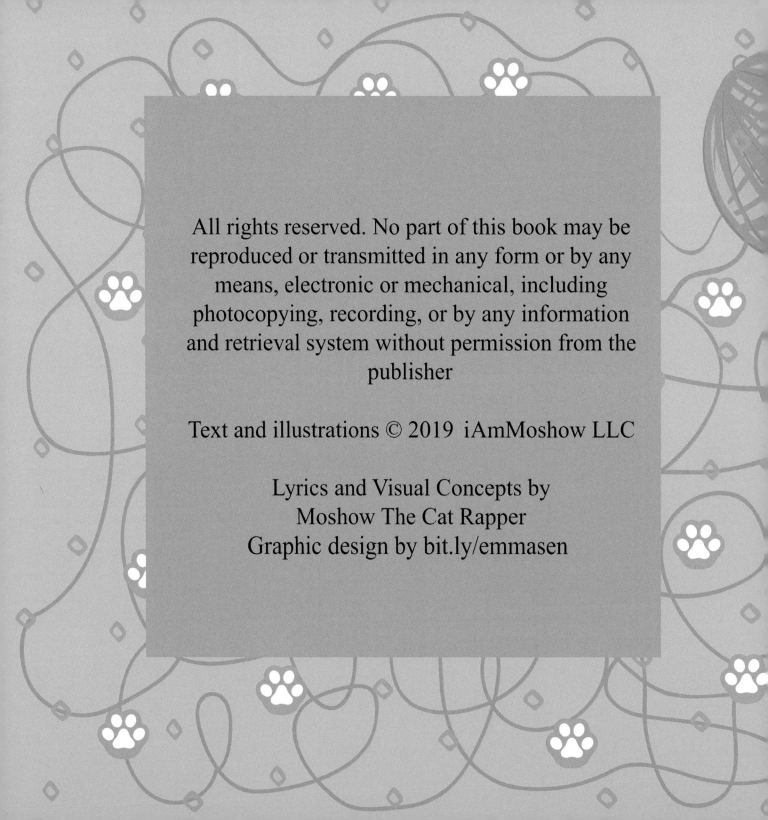

To my adopted son, Black $avage. You've brought me more joy than I could ever imagine.

And to all the cats without homes, I am fighting for you!

Something strange was happening in Moshow's neighborhood. There were homeless cats everywhere!

CATS IN THE BUSHES

... CATS IN THE TREES

Frightened mothers and children ran in every direction because there was no controlling the cats.

Climbing cats and jumping cats...

there were just too many cats!

Moshow worried about all of his cat friends without a home of their own.

The community was upset because the Mayor's plan wasn't working.

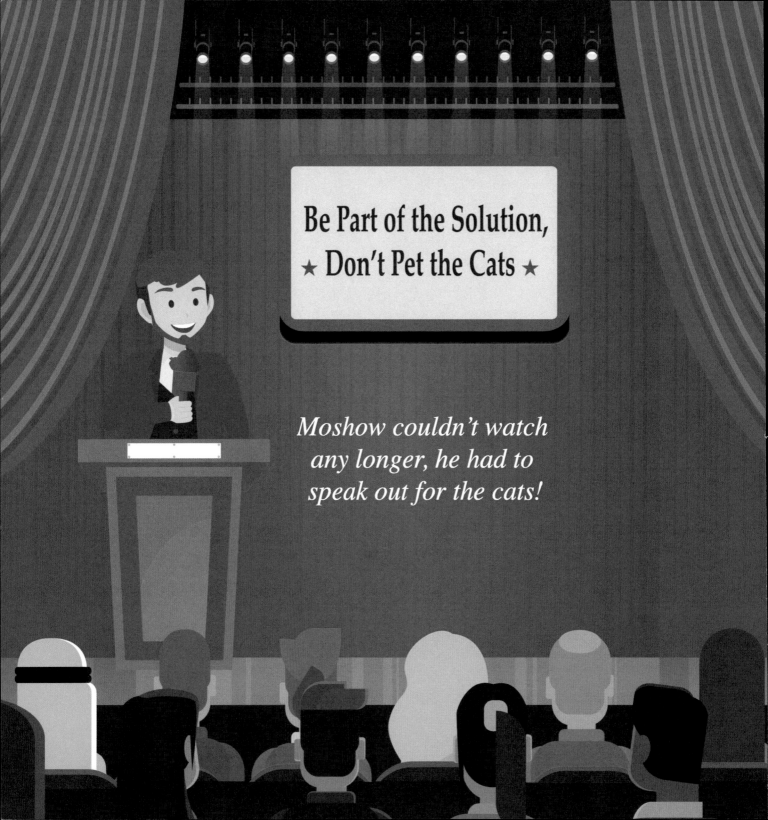

I'm about to adopt a cat
if you ever wonderin where the option's at
I'm about to adopt a cat
Got a bunch of cat love, no stopping that!

Hands up, let's adopt a cat!
Hands up, let's adopt a cat!
Hands up, let's adopt a cat!
Hands up, let's adopt a cat!

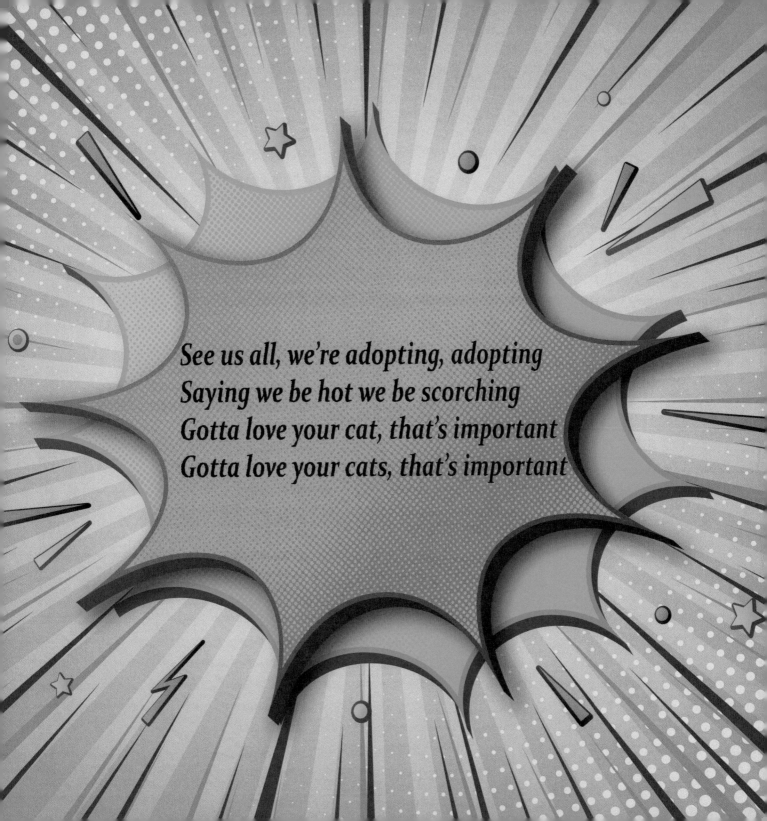

One by one, the cats were finding new homes!

CAT SPA
~~CAT CATCHER~~
~~CITY POUND~~

And soon enough, the Cat Catcher had to find a new way to make a living!

Moshow and his friends found homes for ALL THE CATS!

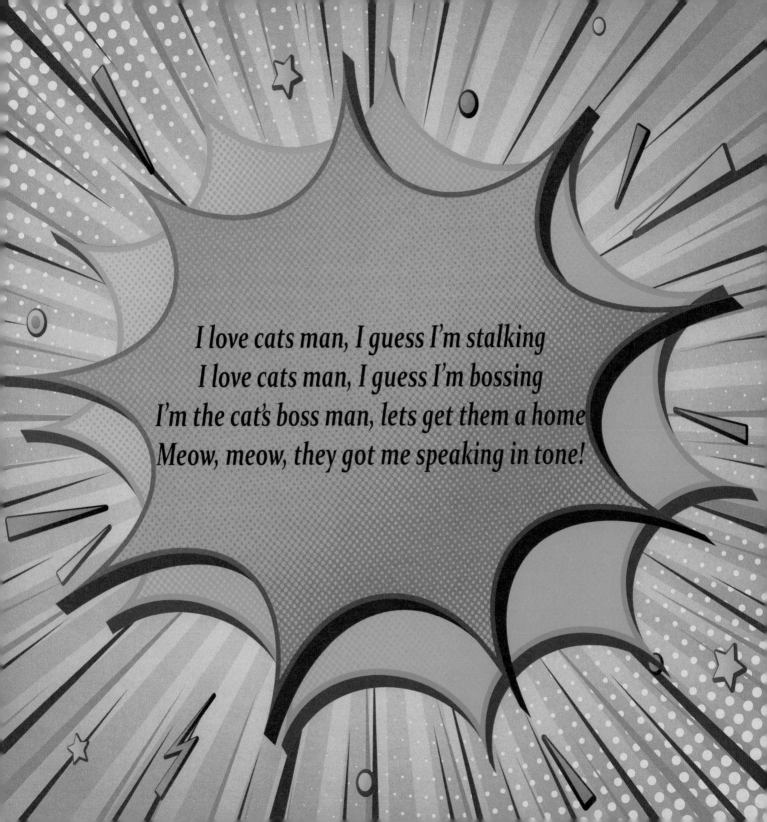

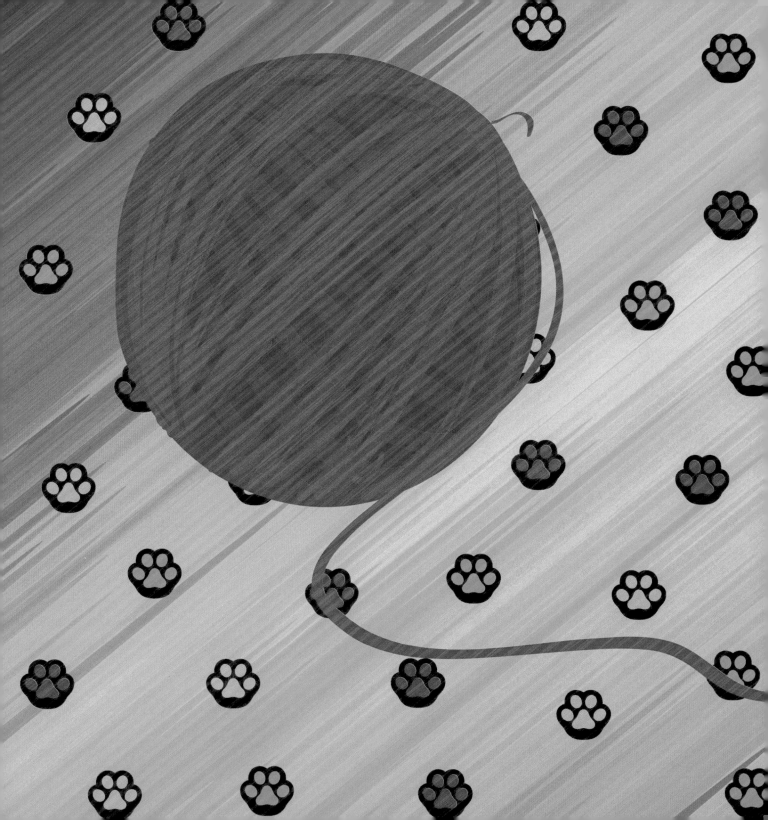

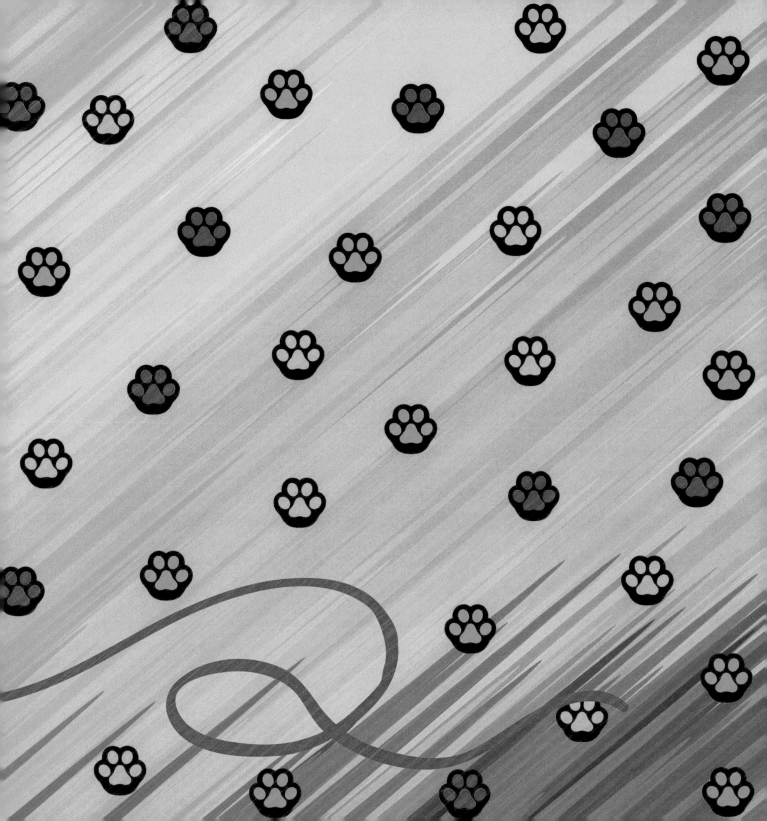

Moshow wants everyone to remember there will always be cats who need a forever home.

Just repeat the words...

You Can Help Save Cats

Moshow the Cat Rapper has long been advocating for the rights of cats, worldwide. He is on a mission to raise awareness of the millions of abused, abandoned and otherwise homeless cats in need of forever homes. Thankfully, there are many hardworking organizations doing their best to remedy the situation. Moshow would like to bring attention to one organization in particular.

Million Cat Challenge

The Million Cat Challenge launched in 2014 as a shelter-based campaign to save the lives of one million cats in North America over five years. When the more than 1,000 participating animal shelters across North America reached and exceeded that goal a full year early, an even bolder goal was conceived: #allthecats.

#allthecats means finding the right outcome for every cat who comes to a shelter, even if that "outcome" is never being admitted at all. It means building the community safety net so that many cats and kittens can get the care they need right where they are. It means providing sufficient space and humane care in the shelter so the cats that do come can be moved quickly and safely to the best possible result: Lost cats go back to their families, cats who have lost their homes are placed in new ones, and cats who are thriving in the community are spayed or neutered and returned to their outdoor home if possible, or placed in a working home if not. And it means that for cats whose suffering can't be remedied any other way, euthanasia will be available with the most kindness and comfort that can possibly be provided.

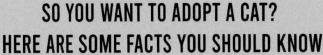
SO YOU WANT TO ADOPT A CAT?
HERE ARE SOME FACTS YOU SHOULD KNOW

Not all cats are the same!

How much time and energy do you have for taking care of your new cat? It's important to remember that not all cats are the same. Bringing home a kitten is a very different experience than bringing home a senior cat. Kittens have a lot of energy and want to play, play, play. Also, make sure you spend time getting to know your cat before you bring her home from the shelter. Just like people, every cat has his or her own personality. Perhaps you want a mellow cat instead of a sassy cat? Just get to know who it is you are bringing home.

Can you afford to care for your cat?

THERE ARE MANY RESPONSIBILITIES RELATED TO CARING FOR A CAT.

Adoption fees can be expensive, but the expense doesn't stop there. Your cat will need toys, kitty litter, collars and leashes, and don't forget about tags and licenses. And finally, you want your cat to stay healthy. Keep in mind regular trips to the vet are very important for your cat's long-term wellness.

Are you ready to bring a cat home?

Make sure you are ready before bringing a cat home. Is your house cat-friendly? Remember, cats like to roam. So make sure you have places for your cat to roll around and play. Variety is the spice of life! Cats get bored just like people do. They love to explore and climb, and you want to make sure they can do that without causing problems in the house.

# Let's go to the vet!

No one really likes going to the doctor, but it's an important fact of life. As soon as you can, you should have your furry friend checked out by a local veterinarian, especially if you have other animals in the house. You want to make sure your cat is healthy and won't bring any sickness into your home.

Do you have any other animals at home?

Do you remember when you met your best friend? Maybe you were a little shy at first? Or maybe you jumped right in and started playing together? Everyone is different. If you have additional pets at home, make sure your new cat isn't stressed out when you introduce her to the rest of the family. Let her explore the house on her own terms, and mingle with the other pets when she is ready. Everyone will get along eventually.

QUESTIONS TO ASK DURING STORYTIME

1. How many of you have kitties of your own at home? What are their names?

2. What is your cat's personality like? Does she have lots of energy? Is he lazy?

3. Do you know what an adoption shelter is? Have you ever been to one?

4. Have you or any of your friends adopted a cat? What was that experience like?

5. What was your favorite part about today's story?

6. Moshow loves music, how about you? Do you know any songs about cats?

Cat facts you can share!

Did you know the average cat sleeps 16-18 hours a day?

A male cat is called a Tom, and a female cat is called a Queen.

Cats can make more than 100 different vocal sounds. Can you make some of these sounds?

Cats have an extremely sensitive sense of smell. 15 times greater than humans, in fact!

Cats greet each other by touching their noses together.

Cats can run up to 30 miles per hour!

A cat's whiskers help them feel their way through dark spaces.

Declawing cats can make them sick, and can cause them to bite.

ADOPT A CAT

by iAmMoshow The Cat Rapper

Na na na na na na na na na naaaaaaa
That's my favorite part - hahaha
Yo, cats need love out here and ummm
Let's a adopt a cat know you what I'm saying If you got
that cat love, let it shine through
You feel me?
MoGang...

I'm about to adopt a cat
If you ever wondering where the options at
I'm about to adopt a cat
Got a bunch of cat love, no stopping that.

I'm about to adopt a cat,
If you ever wondering where the options at
I'm about to adopt a cat,
Got a bunch of cat love, no stopping that.

Hands up, let's adopt a cat!
Hands up, let's adopt a cat!
Hands up, let's adopt a cat!
Hands up, let's adopt a cat!
Hands up, let's adopt a cat!
Hands up, let's adopt a cat!
Hands up, let's adopt a cat!
Hands up, let's adopt a cat!

See us up in Portland, Portland.
Saying we be hot, we be scorching
Gotta love your cat, that's important
Gotta love your cat, that's important

Hands up let's adopt a cat
I'm telling you that's where the options at.

I got a bunch of cat love and I'm hoping that they feel me
They be like, "Do you love cats?" Like, guilty.
This the real me
I'll never fake it.
I love cats man It's really that basic.
Speaking of cats they need a home,
I don't really want them to be alone.
Like home alone
Macaulay Culkin
Let's get these cats they walking,
Walking walking I guess they jogging
I love cats man I guess im stalking
I love cats man I guess I'm bossing
I'm the cats boss man, let's get them a home
Meow, meow they got me speaking in tone.
Flying off the charts so I'm flying in zone.
Cats rule the world so give them the throne,
I know the cat people gotta feel me.

ADOPT A CAT

by iAmMoshow The Cat Rapper

Because I'm just positive man.
Spread a bunch lov,
I said, I said, I said,
I'm just a positive man
And I spread a bunch of cat love.

Meowwwwwwwwwwwww,
Adopt a cat.

I'm about to adopt a cat,
if you ever wondering where the options at.
I'm about to adopt a cat,
Got a bunch of cat love no stopping that.

I'm about to adopt a cat,
if you ever wondering where the options at.
I'm about to adopt a cat,
Got a bunch of cat love no stopping that.

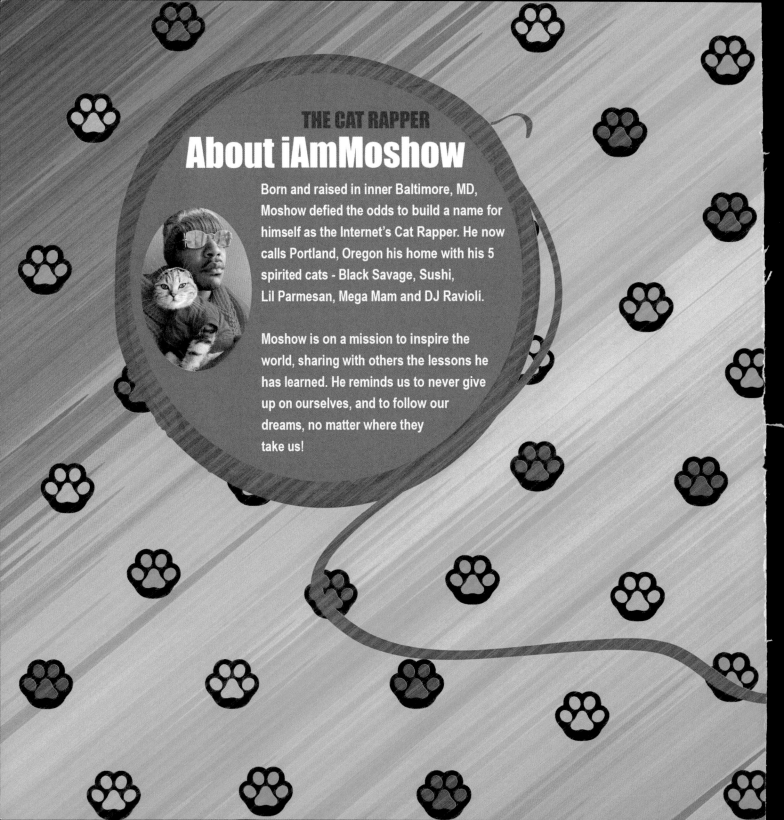

About iAmMoshow

Born and raised in inner Baltimore, MD, Moshow defied the odds to build a name for himself as the Internet's Cat Rapper. He now calls Portland, Oregon his home with his 5 spirited cats - Black Savage, Sushi, Lil Parmesan, Mega Mam and DJ Ravioli.

Moshow is on a mission to inspire the world, sharing with others the lessons he has learned. He reminds us to never give up on ourselves, and to follow our dreams, no matter where they take us!

Made in the USA
San Bernardino, CA
13 June 2020